SUBWAY
CHRISTOPH NIEMANN

GREENWILLOW BOOKS
AN IMPRINT OF
HarperCollins Publishers

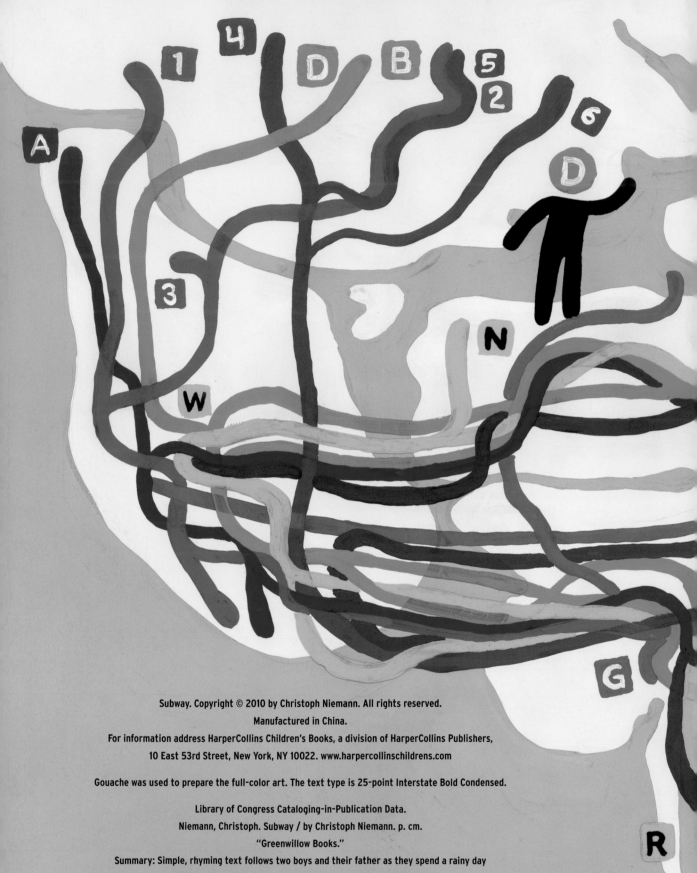

Subway. Copyright © 2010 by Christoph Niemann. All rights reserved.

Manufactured in China.

For information address HarperCollins Children's Books, a division of HarperCollins Publishers,
10 East 53rd Street, New York, NY 10022. www.harpercollinschildrens.com

Gouache was used to prepare the full-color art. The text type is 25-point Interstate Bold Condensed.

Library of Congress Cataloging-in-Publication Data.
Niemann, Christoph. Subway / by Christoph Niemann. p. cm.
"Greenwillow Books."
Summary: Simple, rhyming text follows two boys and their father as they spend a rainy day
riding the various lines of the New York City subway system.
ISBN 978-0-06-157779-6 (trade bdg.) — ISBN 978-0-06-157780-2 (lib. bdg.)
[1. Stories in rhyme. 2. Subways—New York (State)—New York—Fiction.
3. New York (N.Y.)—Fiction. 4. Fathers and sons—Fiction.] I. Title.
PZ8.3.N547Sub 2010   [E]—dc22   2009018756   First Edition
10 11 12 13 14 LEO 10 9 8 7 6 5 4 3 2 1

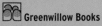 Greenwillow Books

For Arthur, Gustav, and Fritz,
and for my father, Dietmar,
who started it all.

It's cold and wet. What can be done?

A trip on the subway, just for fun!

then a rumble . . .

Hooray!

Here is the first train we'll ride today!

Riding the Ⓐ requires some patience
if you plan to visit all forty-four stations.

INWOOD-207 ST
DYCKMAN ST
190 ST
181 ST
175 ST
168 ST
145 ST
125 ST
59 ST COLUMBUS CIRCLE
42 ST PORT AUTH
34 ST PENN STA
14ST 8 AV
W 4 ST
CANAL ST
CHAMBERS ST
BWAY-NASSAU ST
HIGH ST
JAY ST-BOROUGH HALL
HOYT-SCHERMERHORN
NOSTRAND AV

From Harlem to Brooklyn and Jamaica Bay, then out to the beach at Far Rockaway.

Next up is our favorite train, the F.
We meet a tourist, a banker, a chef.

Witches and cowboys can sometimes be seen
(perhaps not today, but on Halloween).

The 1 train is slow so if you're late, I guess

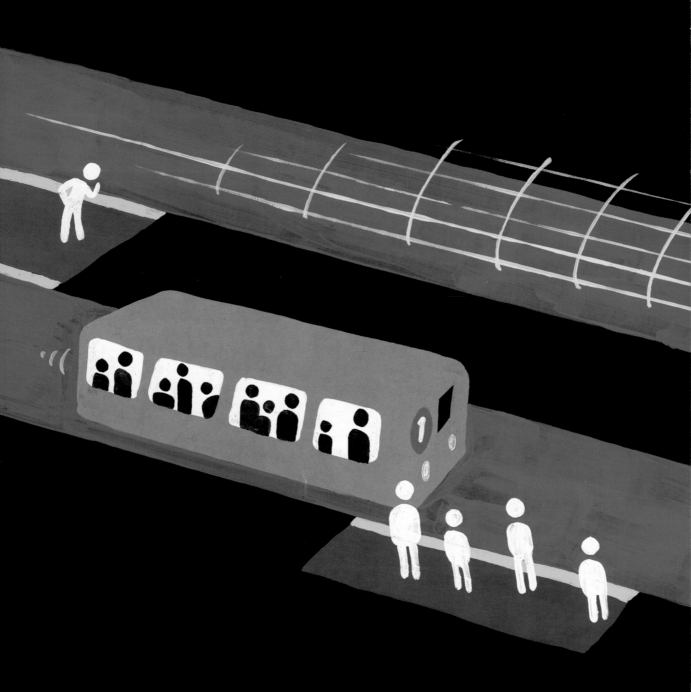

you'd better take the **2**, which runs express.

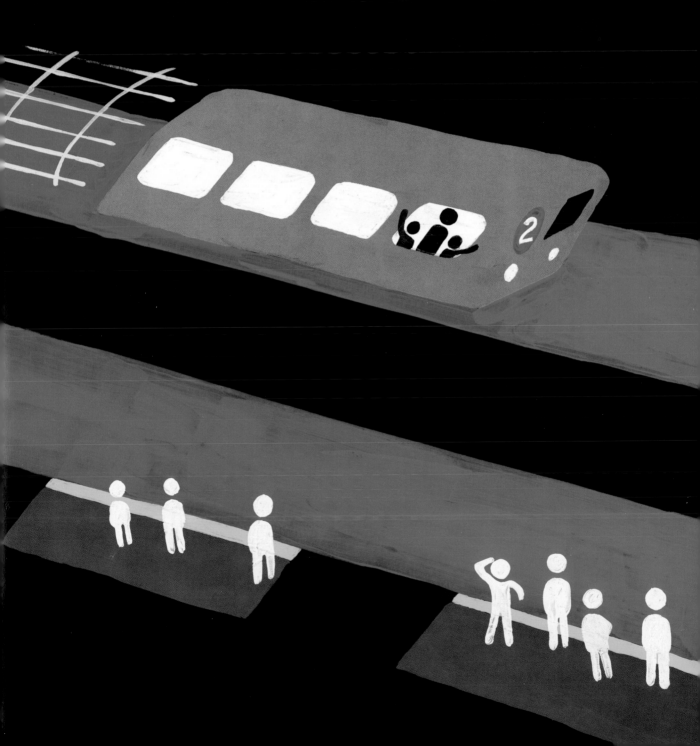

We've tried cars, of course, but finally found

that we much prefer to go underground.

The ⑦ is on his way to meet . . .

his friends at
Times Square, 42nd Street!

enjoying the subway
all night and all day.

At Bergen the F is sad to see
he has to separate from his friend the G.

The G says, "Don't cry. I will meet you again at Roosevelt Avenue!"

we could go straight but we are sure

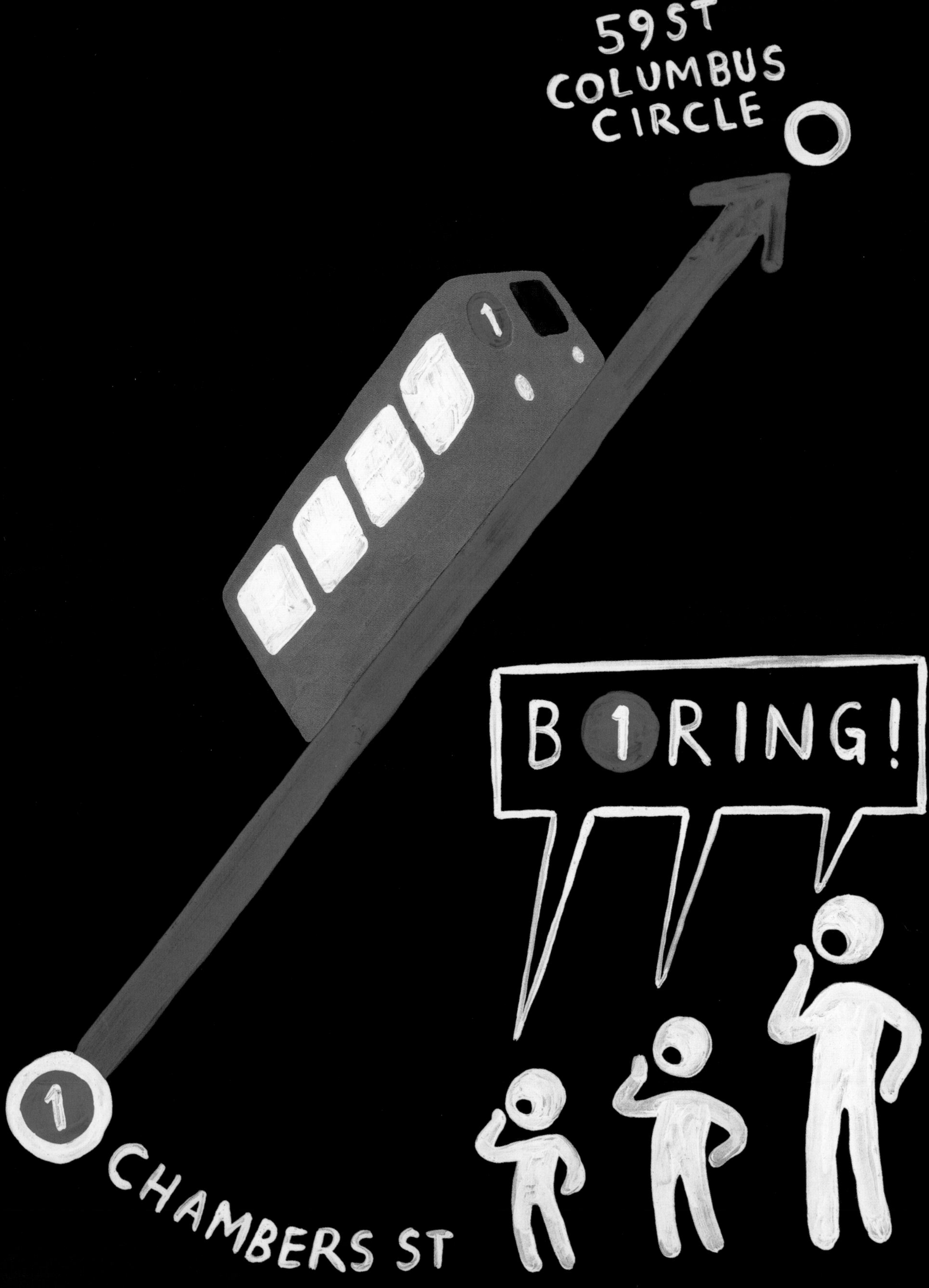

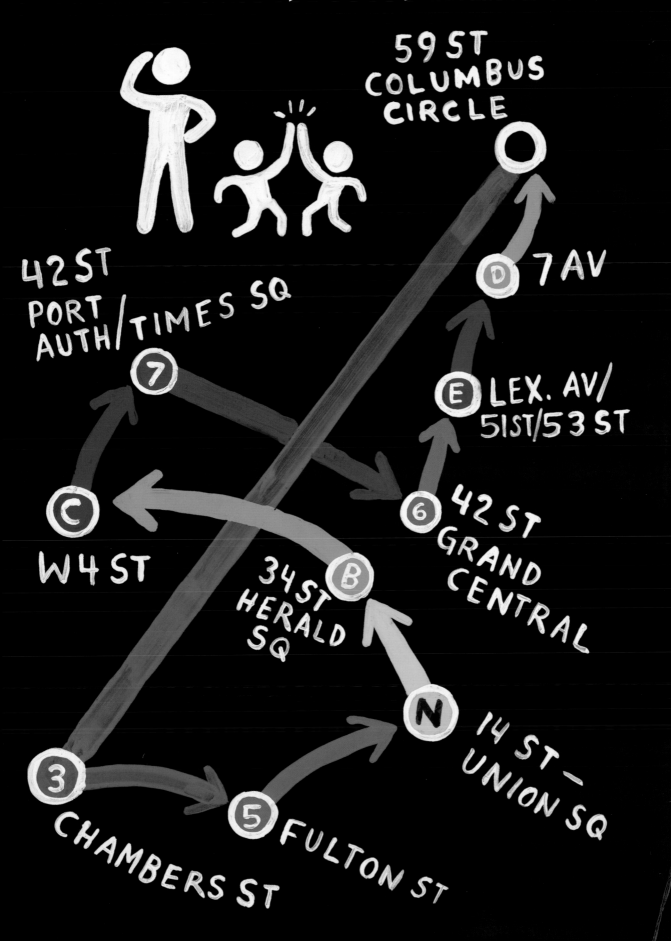

as Daddy drags us off the train.

Now we're turning out the light.

we'll have subway dreams tonight!